# Little Dinosaur, The Hero

by Michèle Dufresne

Illustrations by Sterling Lamet

PIONEER VALLEY EDUCATIONAL PRESS, INC.

One day Baby Skunk
was playing by the river.
"Look at this!" said Baby Skunk.
"I have a boat!"

Baby Skunk began to go
down the river in his boat.
"Oh, no!" said Baby Skunk.
"Help! I am going down the river!"

"Someone is calling for help," said Monkey.

"Come on," said Little Dinosaur. "Let's see if we can help."

Monkey and Little Dinosaur
ran to the river.
They saw Baby Skunk
going down the river in his boat.

Mother Skunk ran up.

"Oh, no," she said.

"Baby Skunk!

Baby Skunk is going down the river.

Oh, dear! Oh, dear!

I can't swim!"

"I can swim," said Little Dinosaur.
He jumped into the water
and began to swim.
"I'm coming," he shouted
to Baby Skunk.
"Here I come!"

"Get on my back," said Little Dinosaur. "Get on my back, and I will take you to Mother Skunk."

"Thank you, Little Dinosaur,"
said Mother Skunk.
"You're a hero!"